W9-CMZ-973

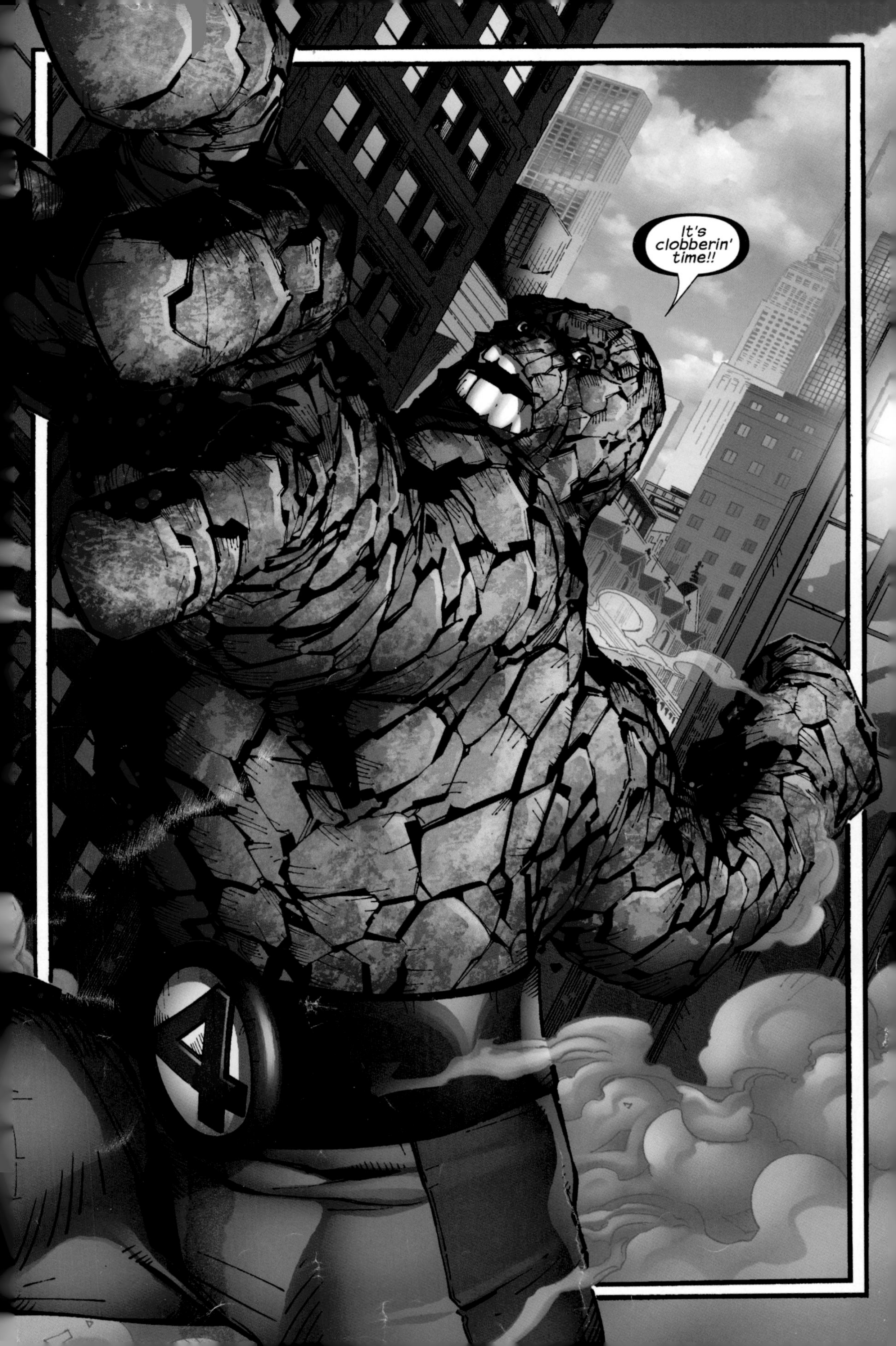
It's clobberin' time!!

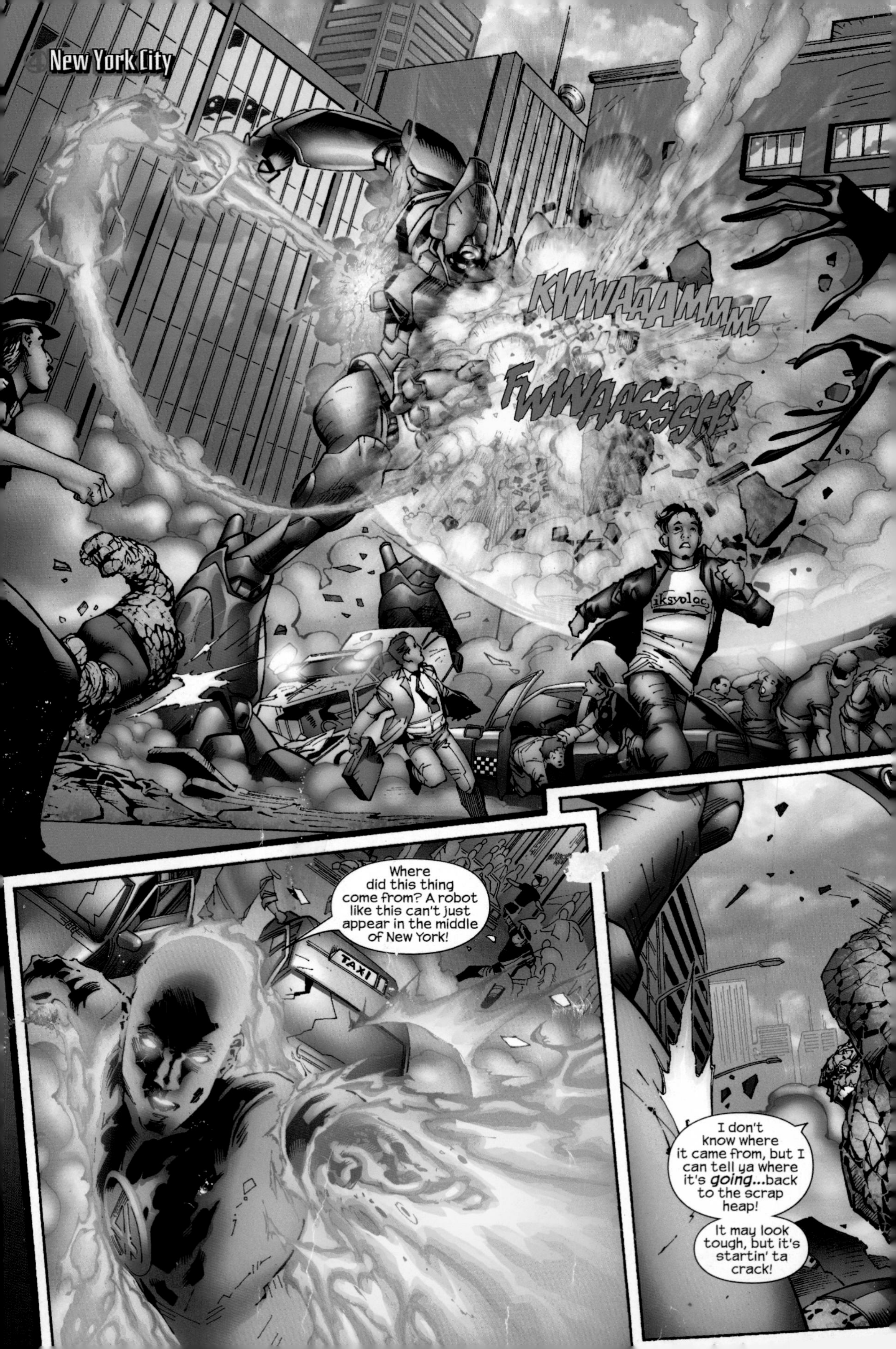
New York City
KWWAAAMMMM!
FWWAASSSH!
iksyolac
TAXI
Where did this thing come from? A robot like this can't just appear in the middle of New York!
I don't know where it came from, but I can tell ya where it's *going*...back to the scrap heap!
It may look tough, but it's startin' ta crack!

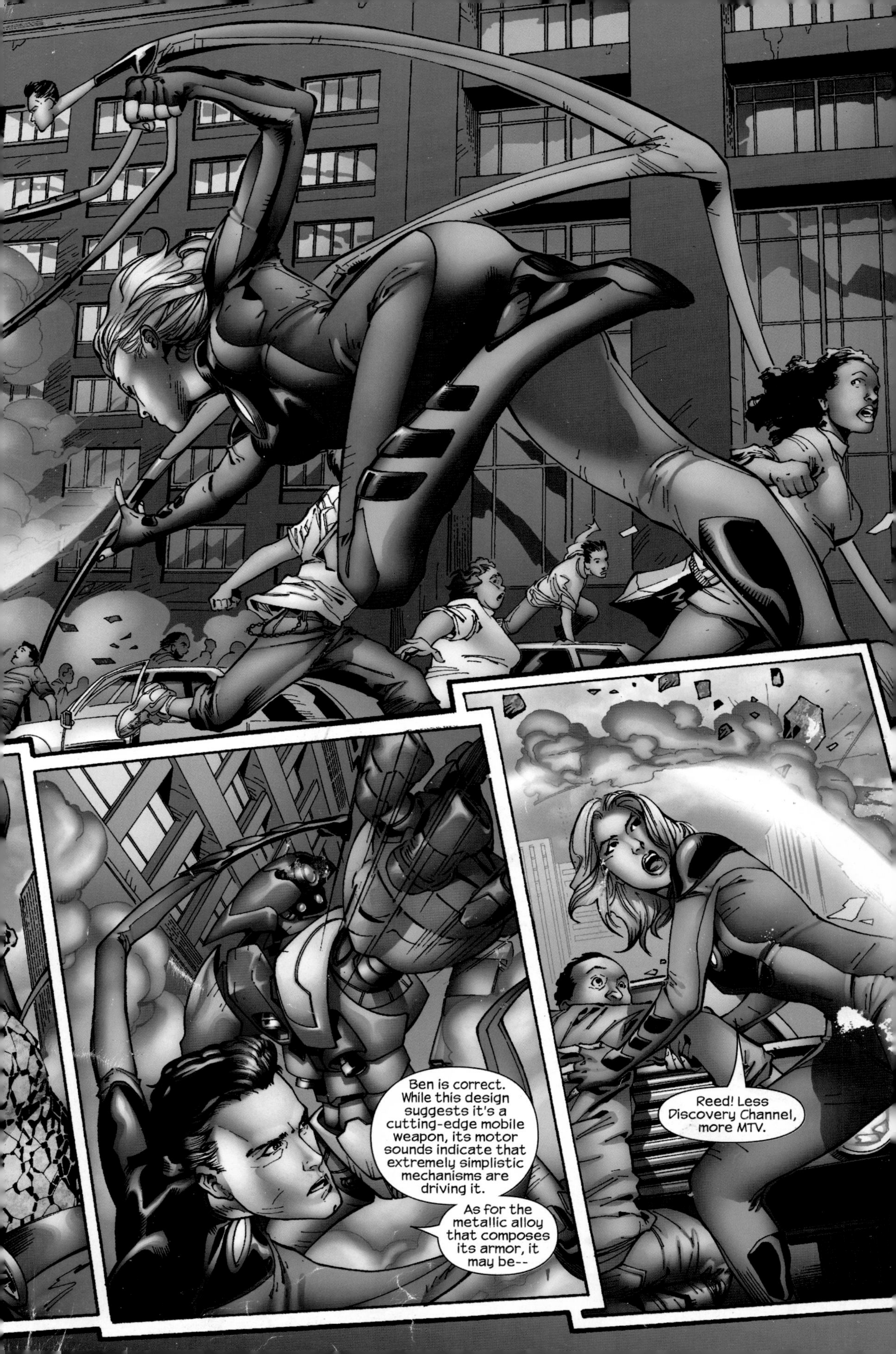

Ben is correct. While this design suggests it's a cutting-edge mobile weapon, its motor sounds indicate that extremely simplistic mechanisms are driving it.
As for the metallic alloy that composes its armor, it may be--
Reed! Less Discovery Channel, more MTV.

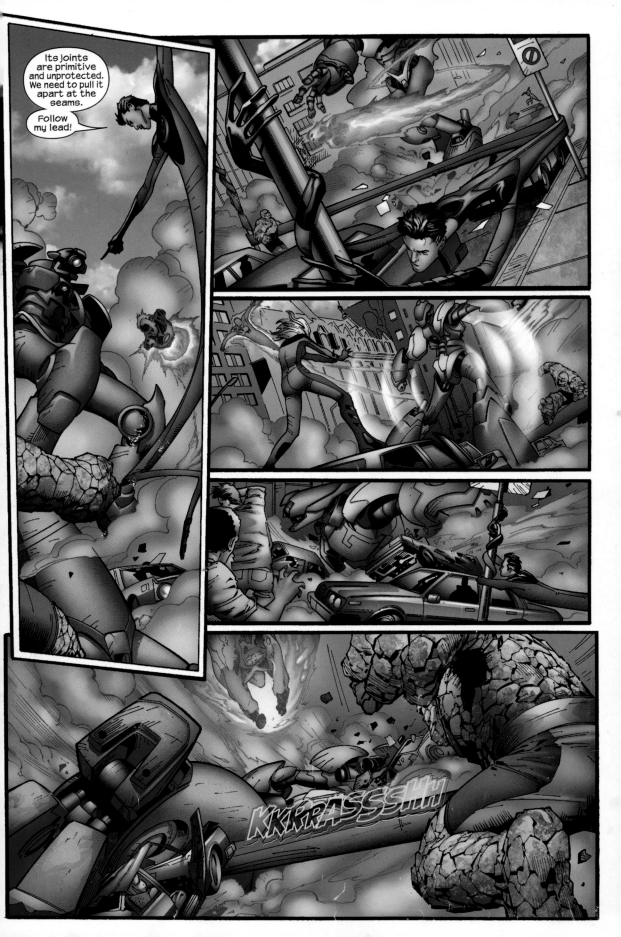

Its joints are primitive and unprotected. We need to pull it apart at the seams.

Follow my lead!

KKRRASSSHH!!

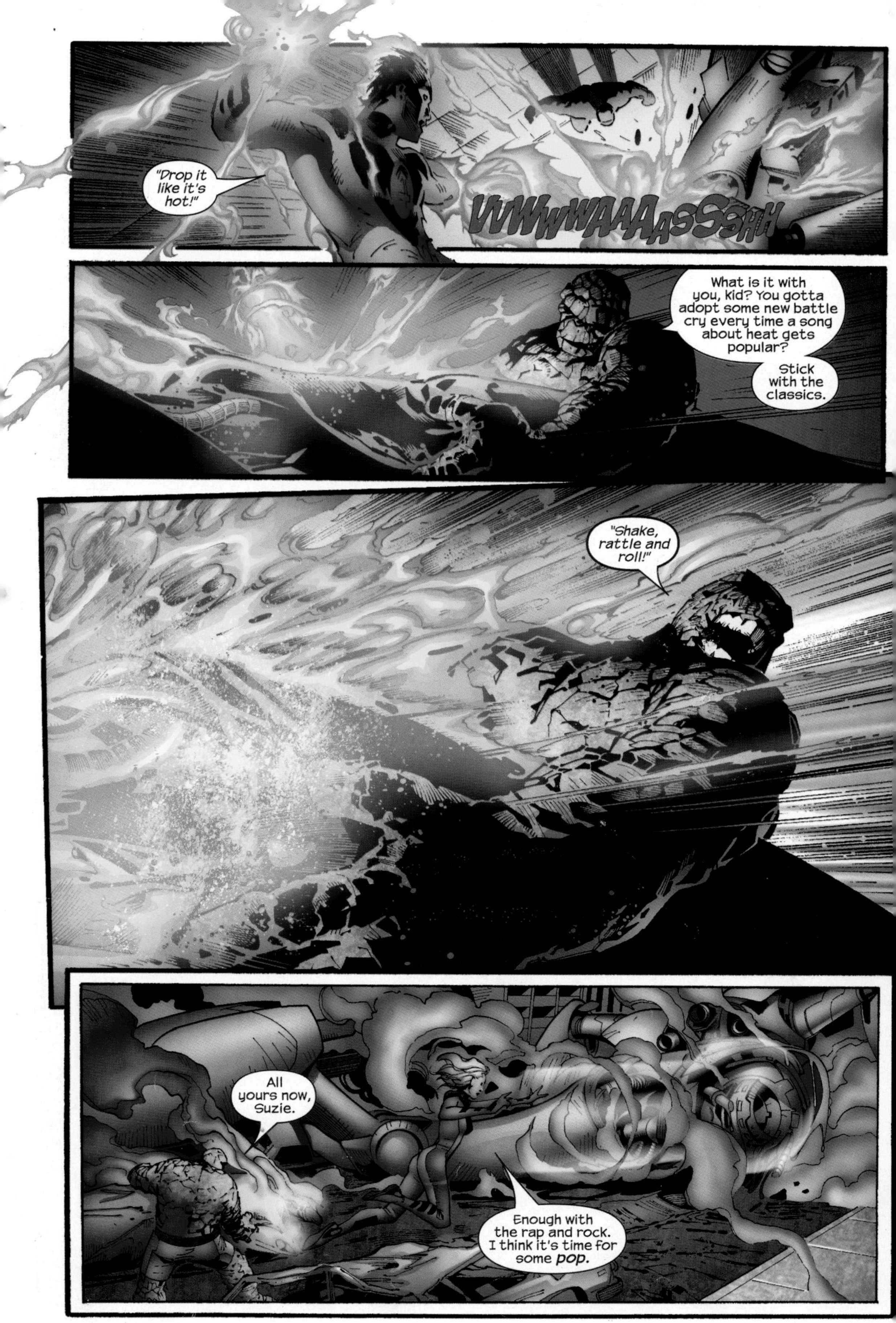
"Drop it like it's hot!"
VVWWWAAAAASSSHH
What is it with you, kid? You gotta adopt some new battle cry every time a song about heat gets popular?
Stick with the classics.
"Shake, rattle and roll!"
All yours now, Suzie.
Enough with the rap and rock. I think it's time for some *pop*.

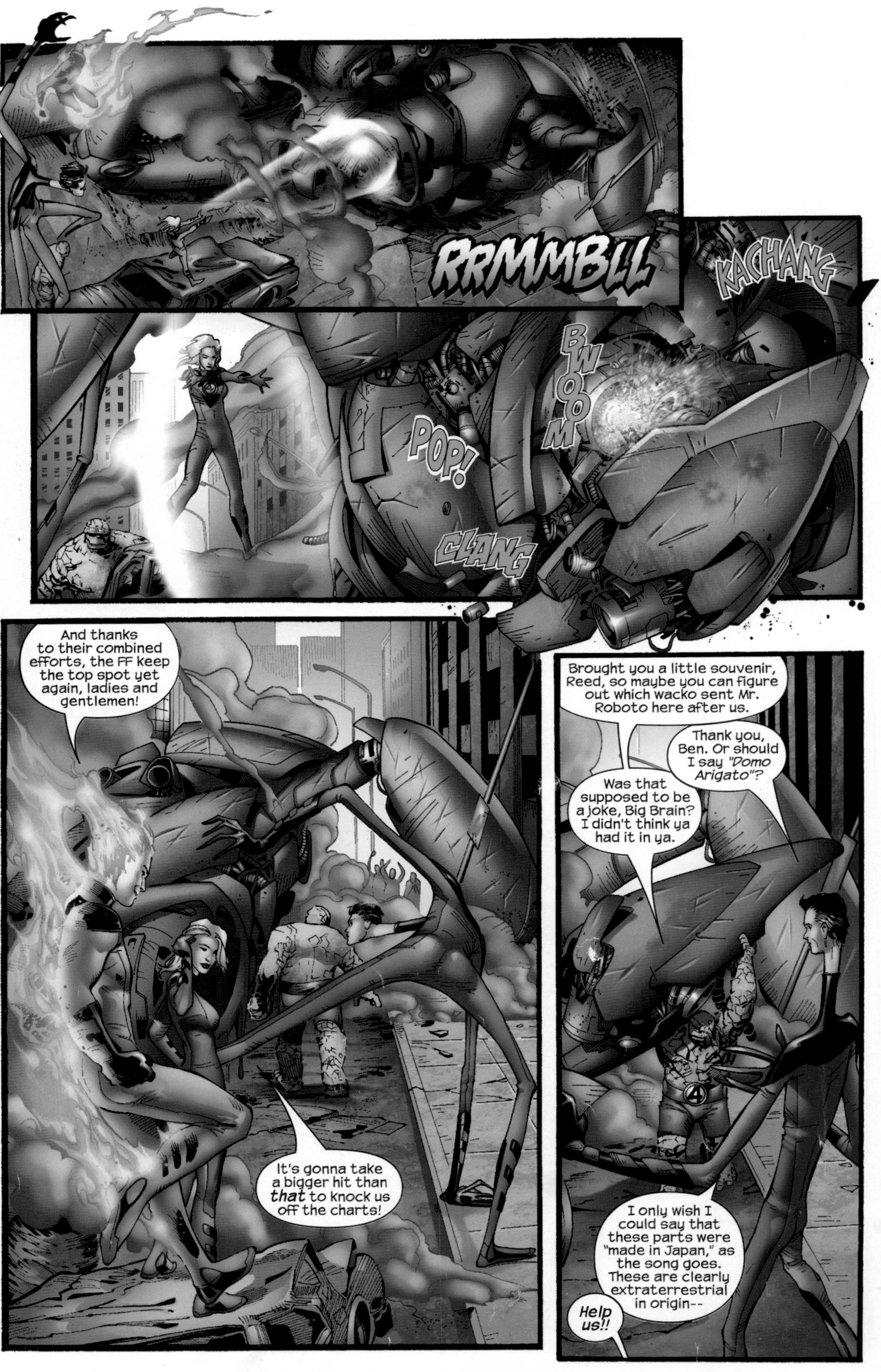
RRMMBLL
KACHANG
BWOOOM
POP!
CLANG
And thanks to their combined efforts, the FF keep the top spot yet again, ladies and gentlemen!
It's gonna take a bigger hit than *that* to knock us off the charts!
Brought you a little souvenir, Reed, so maybe you can figure out which wacko sent Mr. Roboto here after us.
Thank you, Ben. Or should I say *"Domo Arigato"*?
Was that supposed to be a joke, Big Brain? I didn't think ya had it in ya.
I only wish I could say that these parts were "made in Japan," as the song goes. These are clearly extraterrestrial in origin--
Help us!!

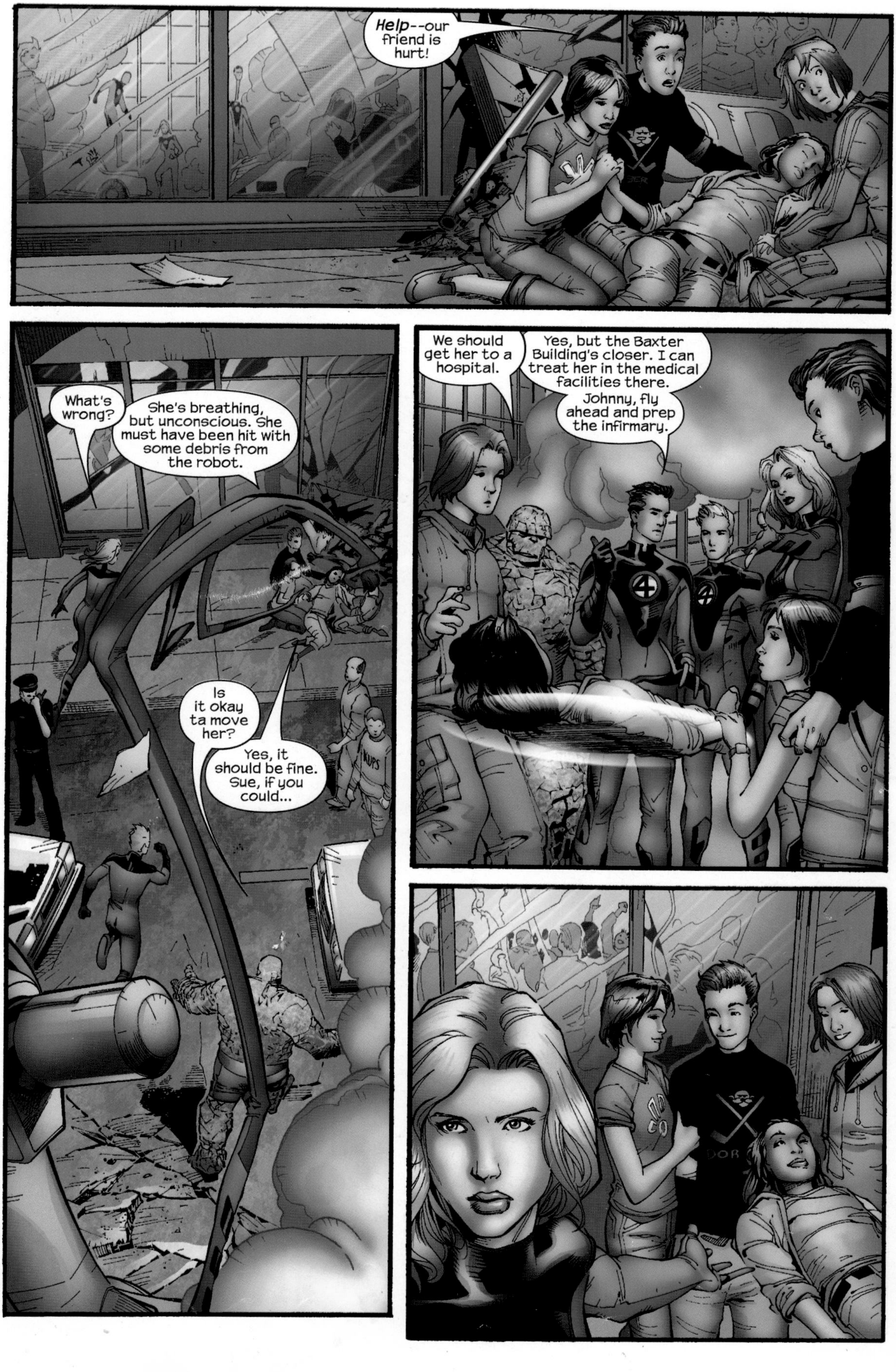
Help--our friend is hurt!
What's wrong?
She's breathing, but unconscious. She must have been hit with some debris from the robot.
Is it okay ta move her?
Yes, it should be fine. Sue, if you could...
We should get her to a hospital.
Yes, but the Baxter Building's closer. I can treat her in the medical facilities there.
Johnny, fly ahead and prep the infirmary.

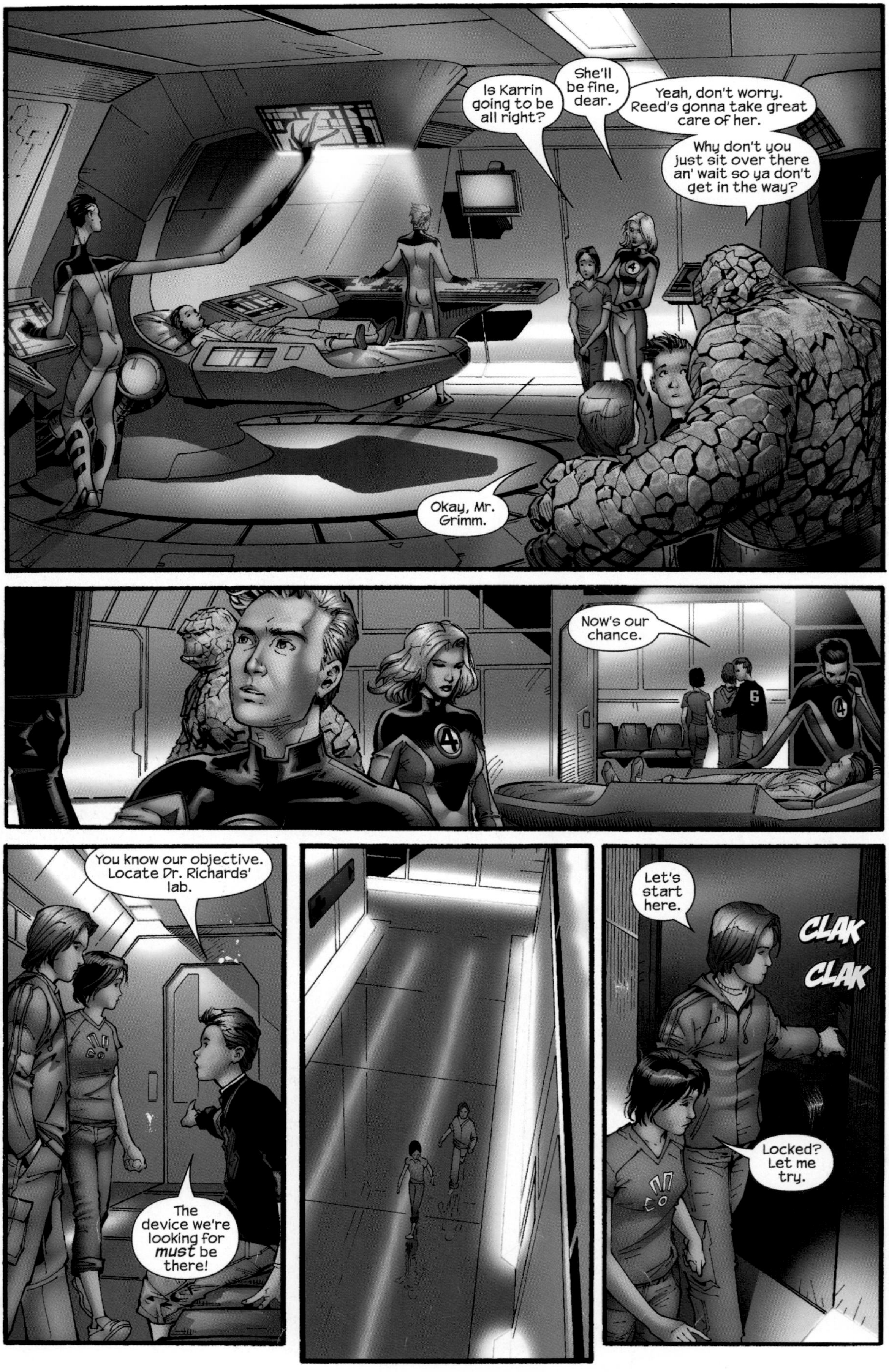
Is Karrin going to be all right?
She'll be fine, dear.
Yeah, don't worry. Reed's gonna take great care of her.
Why don't you just sit over there an' wait so ya don't get in the way?
Okay, Mr. Grimm.
Now's our chance.
You know our objective. Locate Dr. Richards' lab.
The device we're looking for *must* be there!
Let's start here.
CLAK
CLAK
Locked? Let me try.

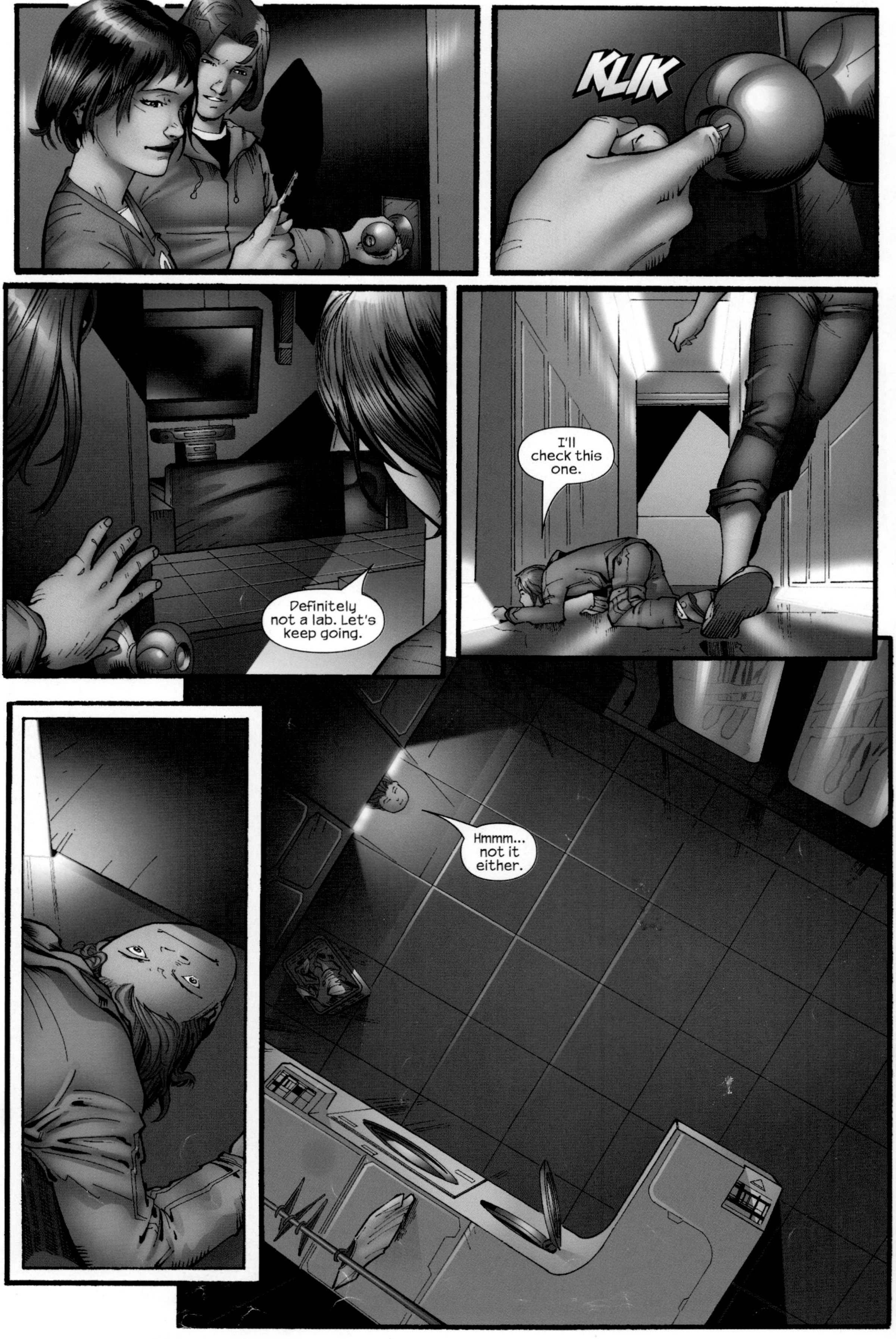
KLIK
Definitely not a lab. Let's keep going.
I'll check this one.
Hmmm... not it either.

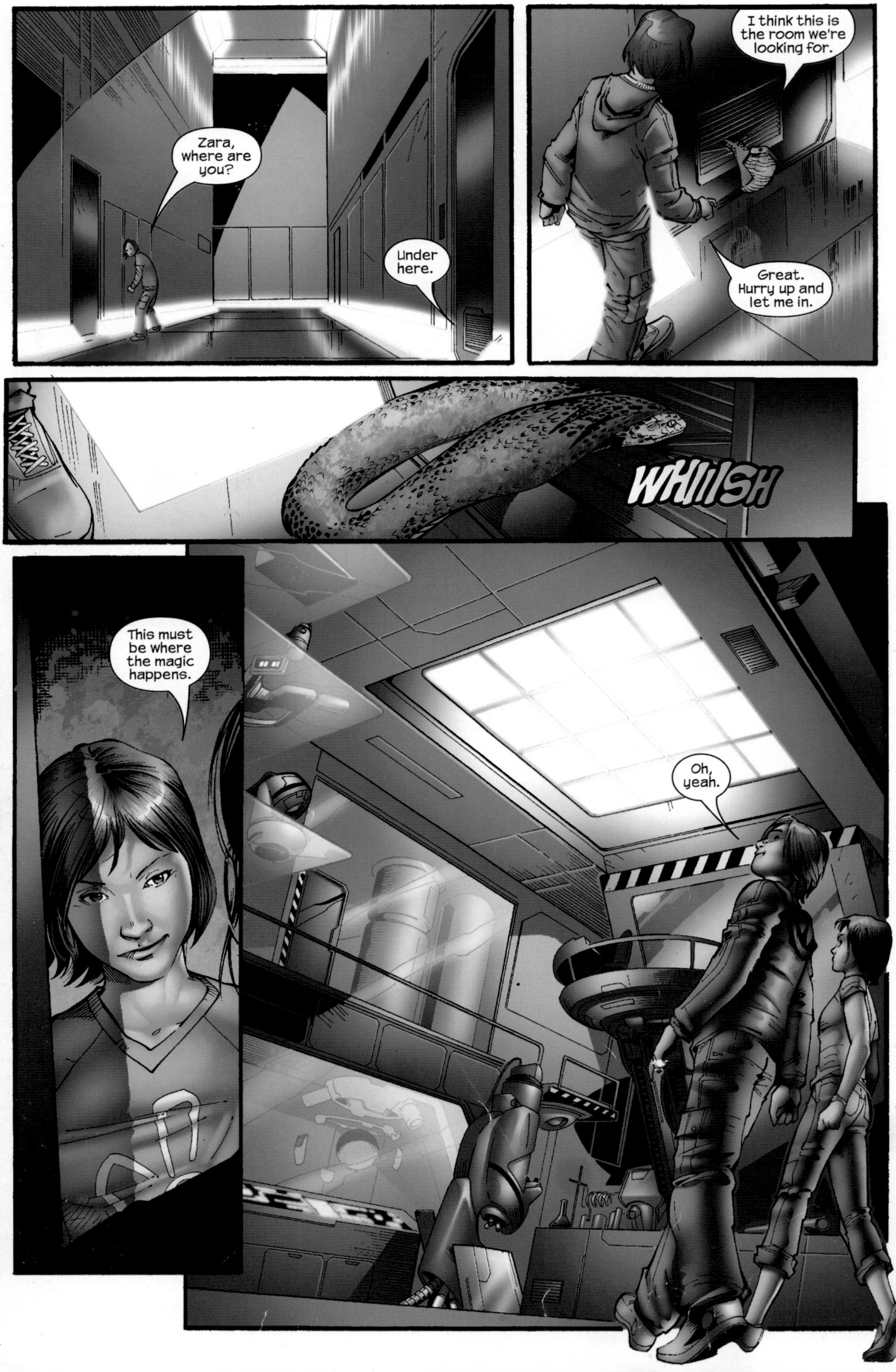
Zara, where are you?
Under here.
I think this is the room we're looking for.
Great. Hurry up and let me in.
WHIIISH
This must be where the magic happens.
Oh, yeah.

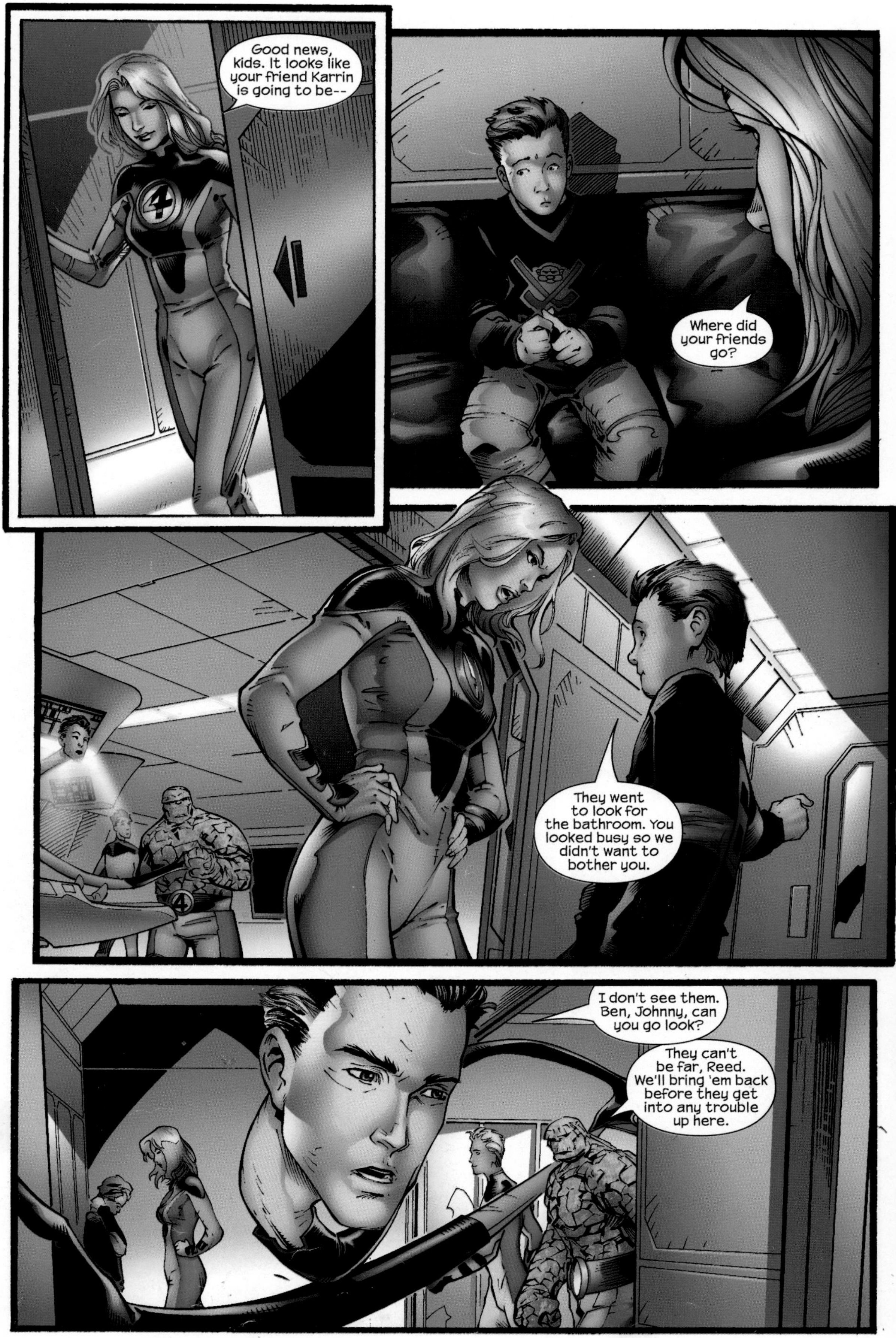

Good news, kids. It looks like your friend Karrin is going to be--
Where did your friends go?
They went to look for the bathroom. You looked busy so we didn't want to bother you.
I don't see them. Ben, Johnny, can you go look?
They can't be far, Reed. We'll bring 'em back before they get into any trouble up here.

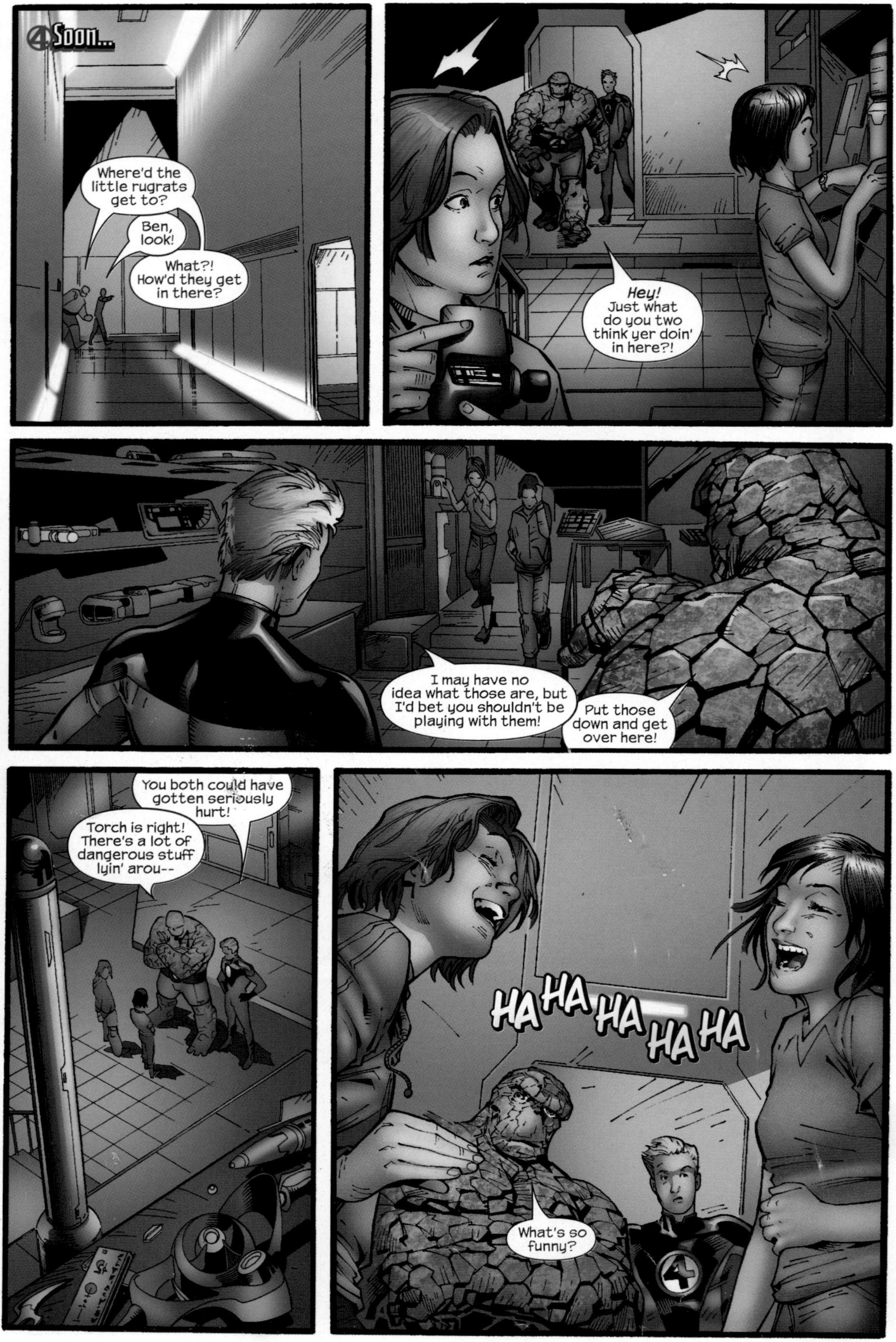

Soon...
Where'd the little rugrats get to?
Ben, look!
What?! How'd they get in there?
Hey! Just what do you two think yer doin' in here?!
I may have no idea what those are, but I'd bet you shouldn't be playing with them!
Put those down and get over here!
You both could have gotten seriously hurt!
Torch is right! There's a lot of dangerous stuff lyin' arou--
HA HA HA HA HA HA
What's so funny?

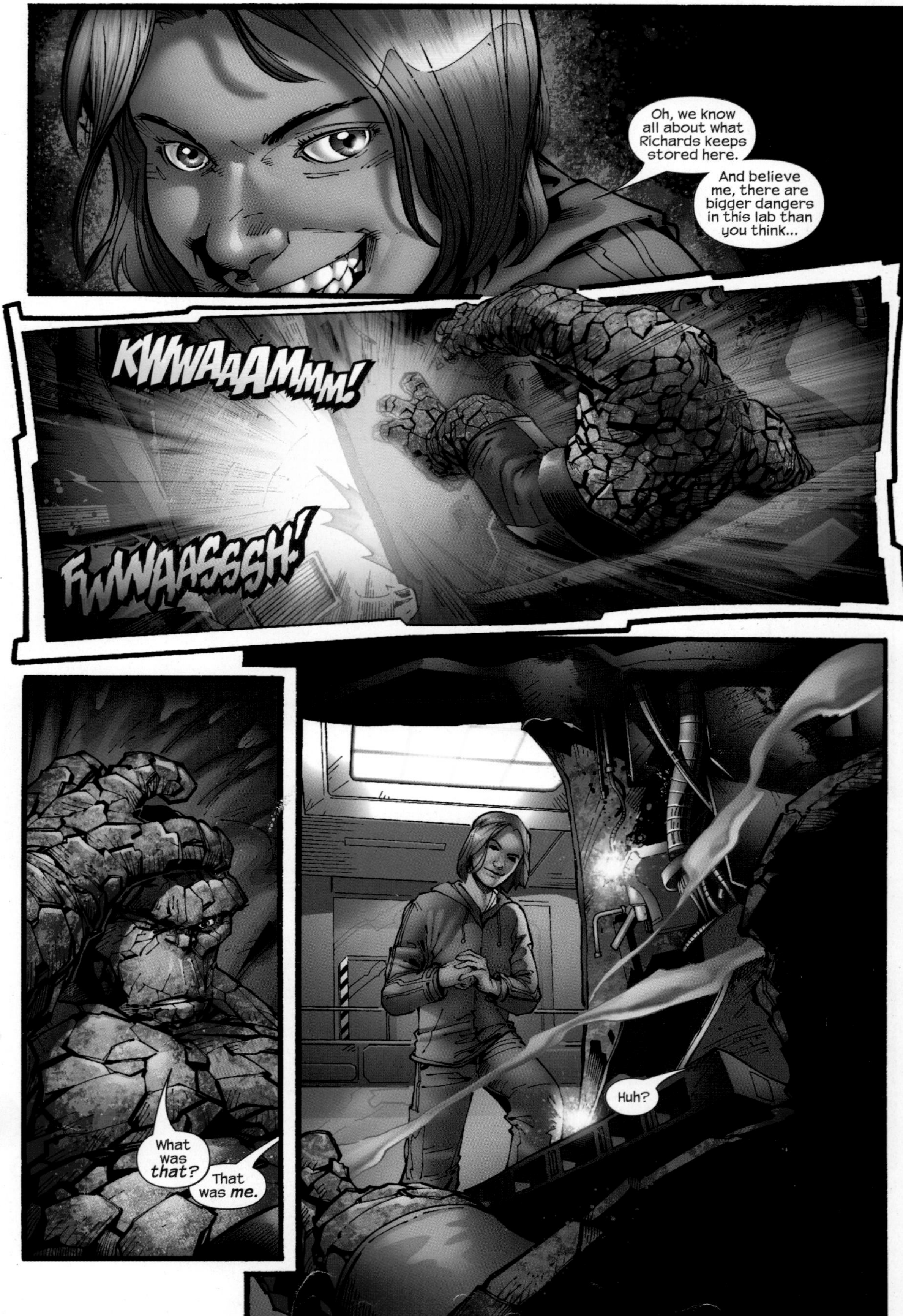

Oh, we know all about what Richards keeps stored here.
And believe me, there are bigger dangers in this lab than you think...
KWWAAAMMMM!
FWWAASSSH!
What was *that*?
That was *me*.
Huh?

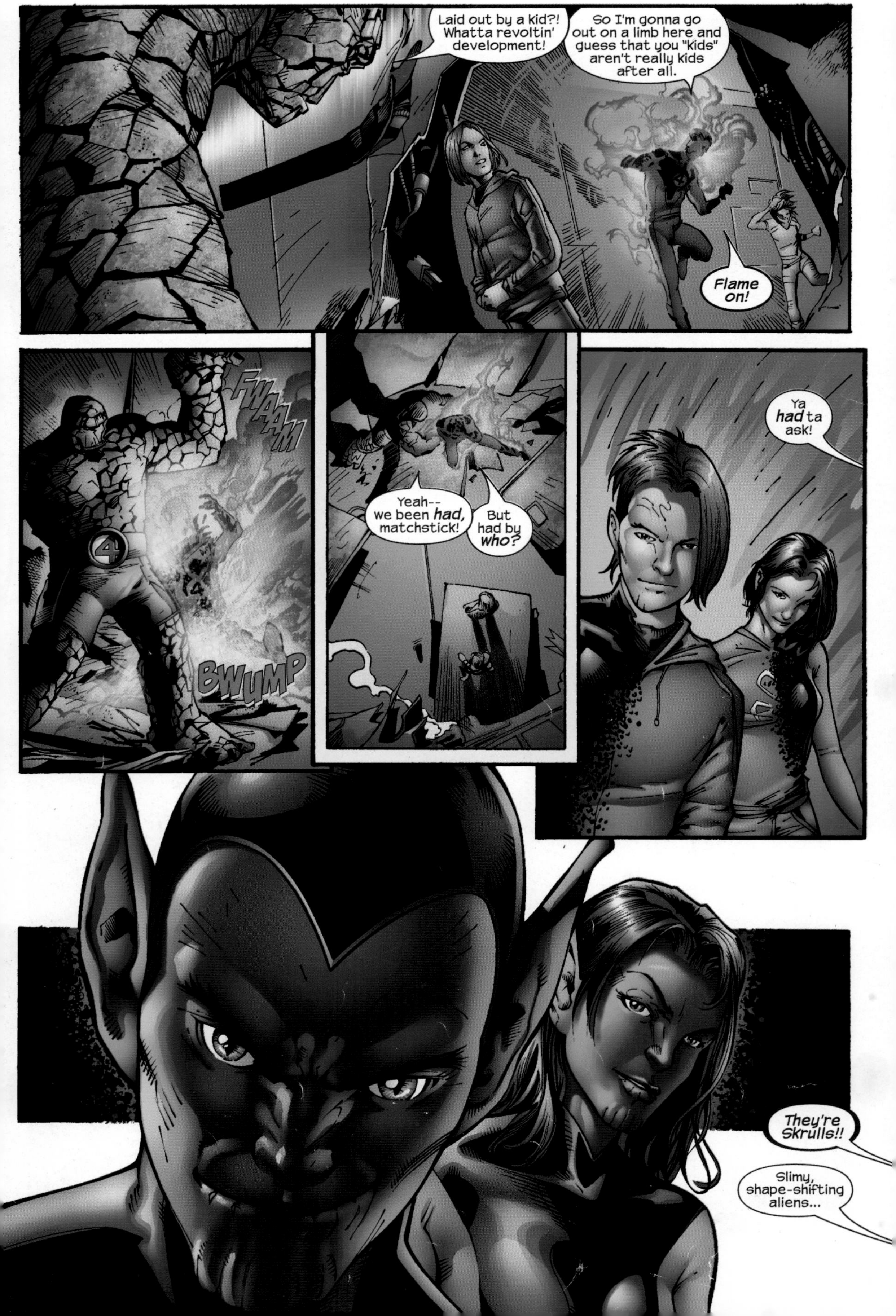
Laid out by a kid?! Whatta revoltin' development!
So I'm gonna go out on a limb here and guess that you "kids" aren't really kids after all.
Flame on!
FWAAM
BWUMP
Yeah-- we been *had,* matchstick!
But had by *who?*
Ya *had* ta ask!
They're Skrulls!!
Slimy, shape-shifting aliens...

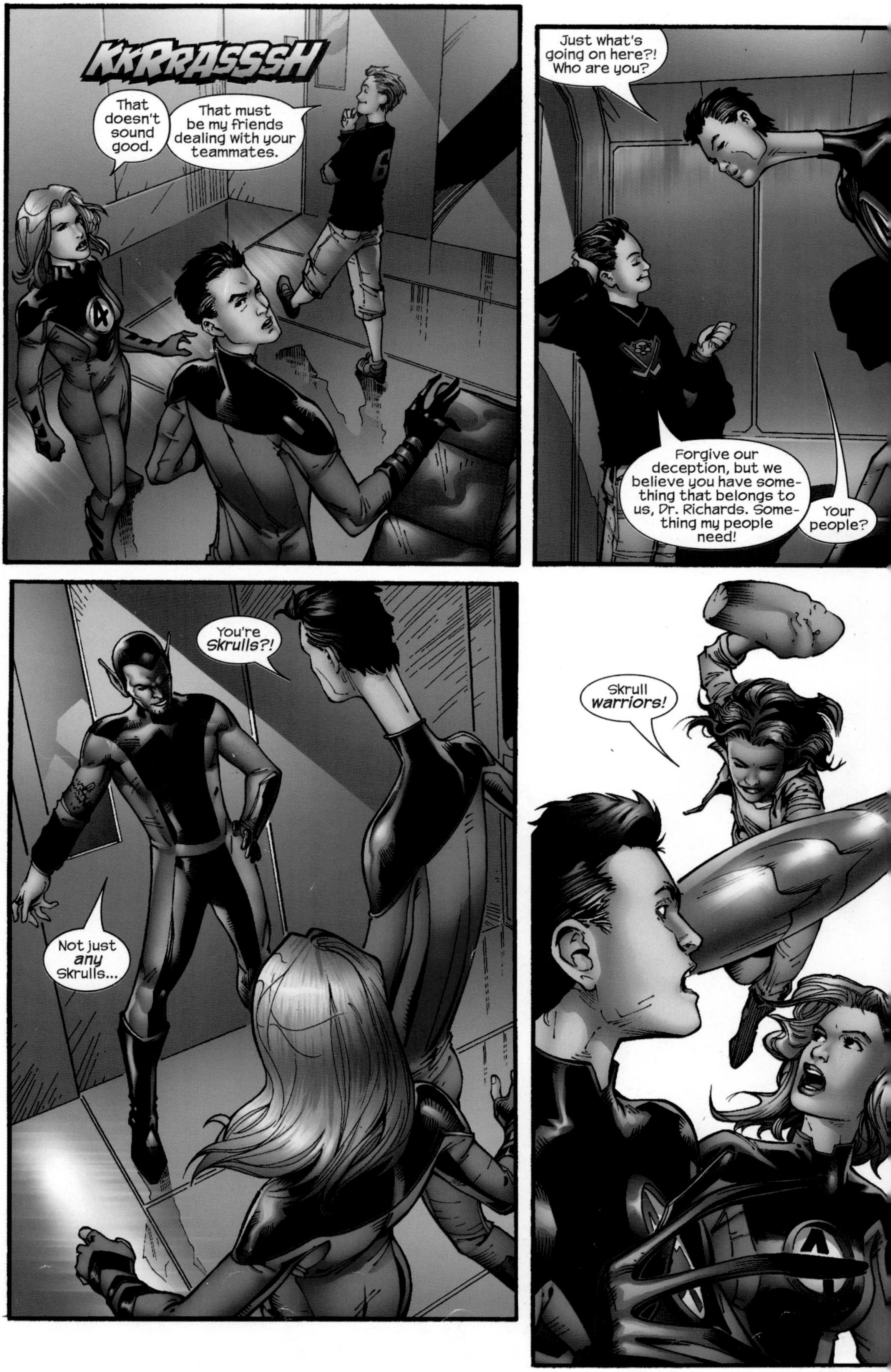
KKRRASSSH
That doesn't sound good.
That must be my friends dealing with your teammates.
Just what's going on here?! Who are you?
Forgive our deception, but we believe you have something that belongs to us, Dr. Richards. Something my people need!
Your people?
You're Skrulls?!
Not just any Skrulls...
Skrull warriors!

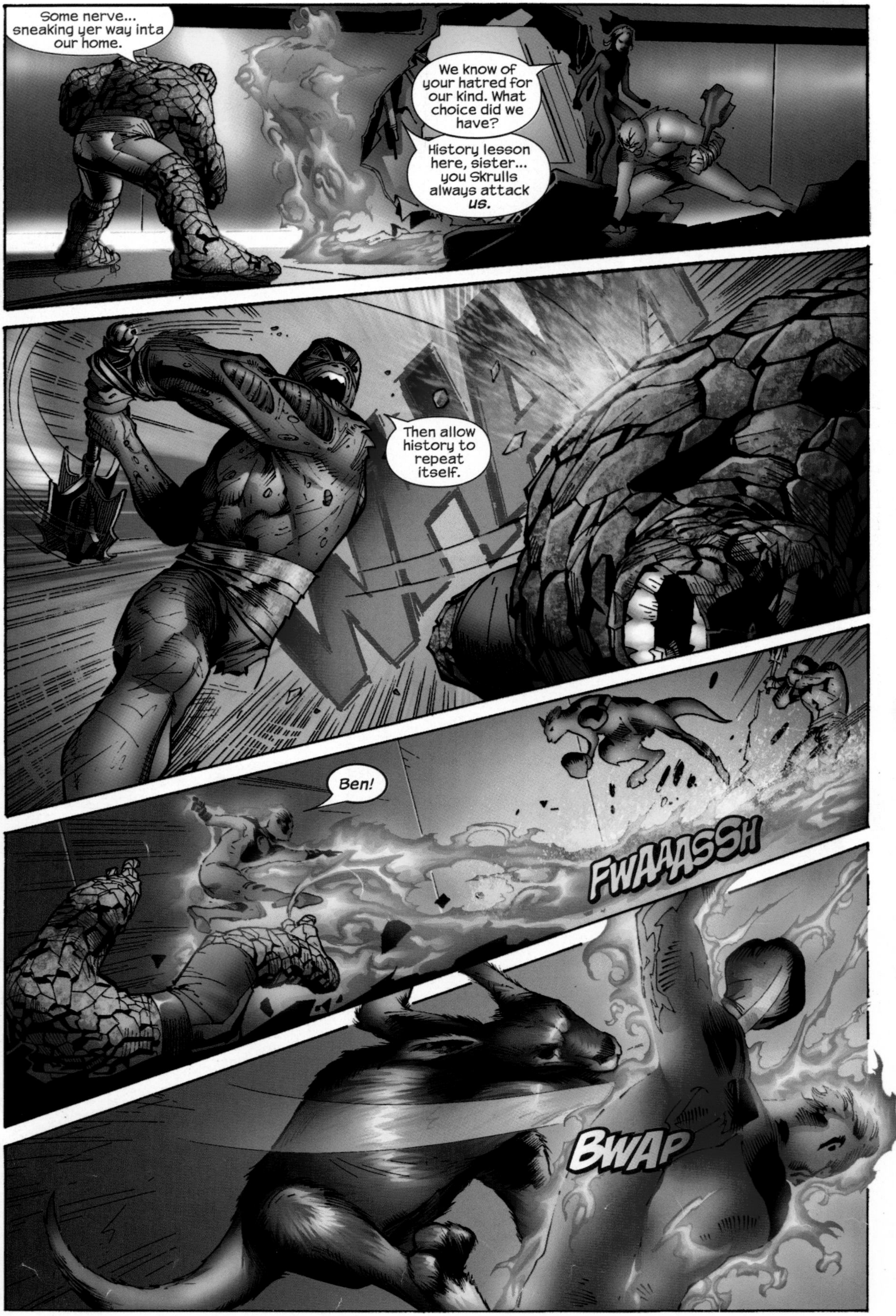

Some nerve... sneaking yer way inta our home.
We know of your hatred for our kind. What choice did we have?
History lesson here, sister... you Skrulls always attack *us.*
Then allow history to repeat itself.
Ben!
FWAAASSH
BWAP

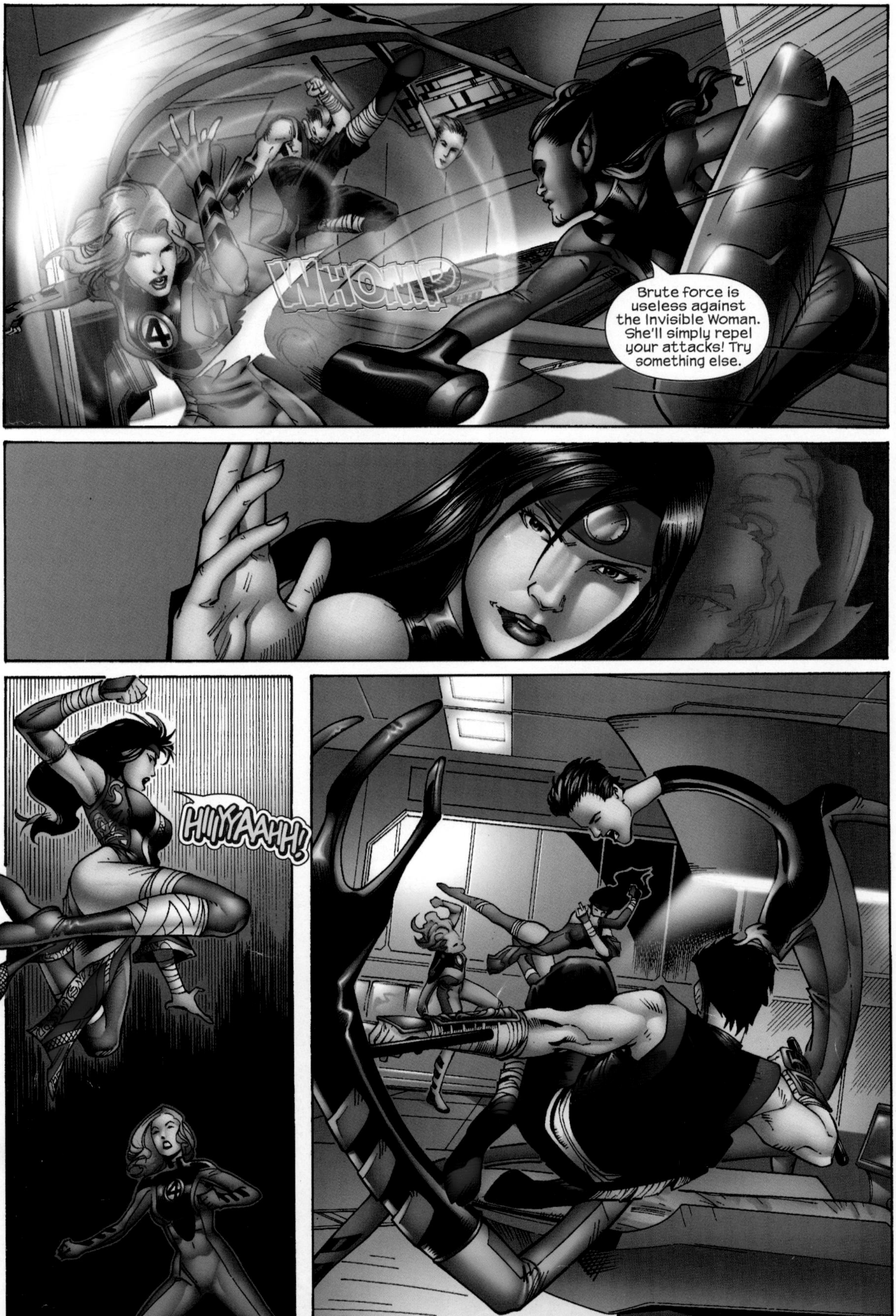
WHOMP
Brute force is useless against the Invisible Woman. She'll simply repel your attacks! Try something else.
HIIIYAAHH!

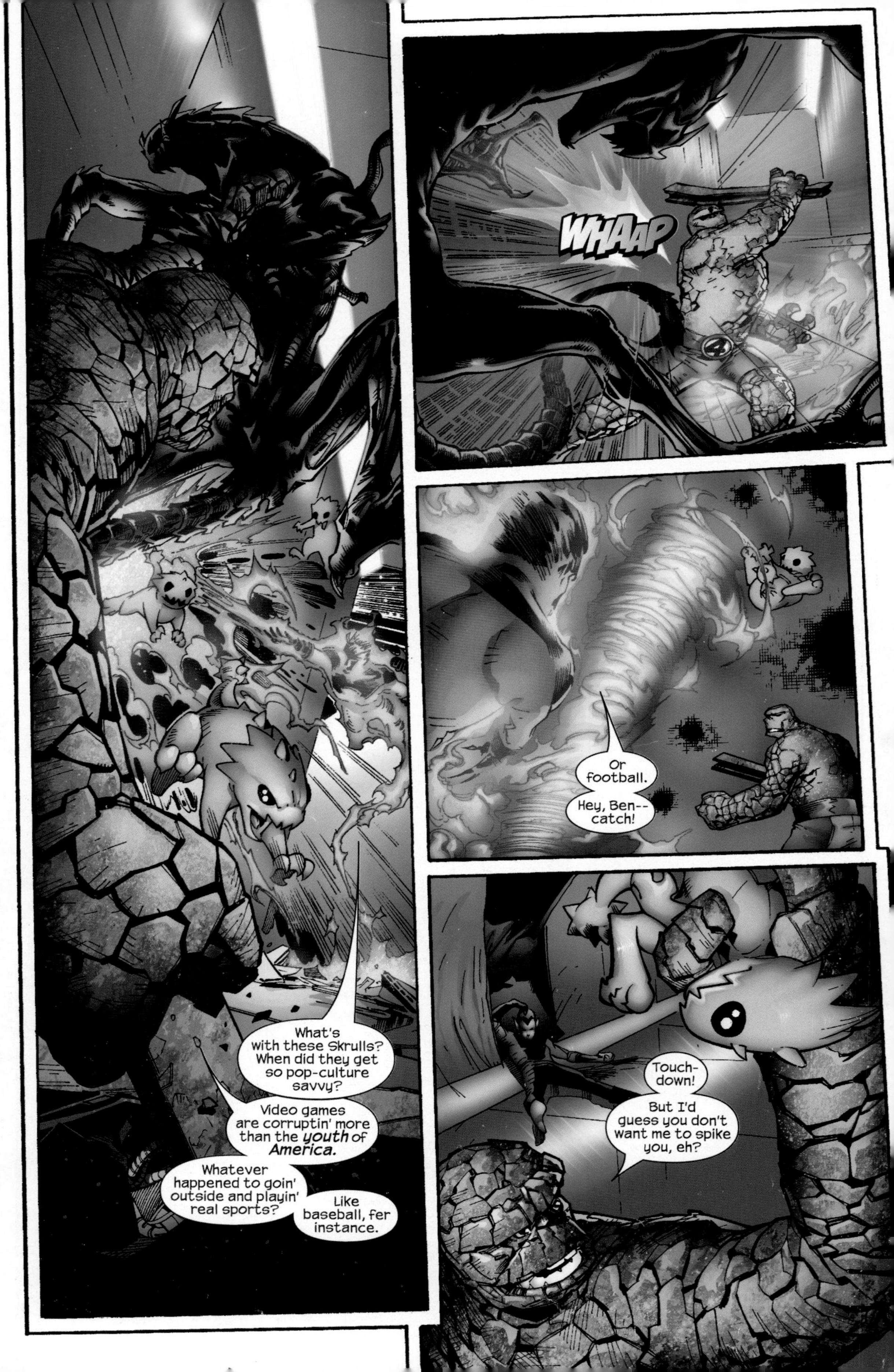

What's with these Skrulls? When did they get so pop-culture savvy?
Video games are corruptin' more than the *youth* of *America.*
Whatever happened to goin' outside and playin' real sports?
Like baseball, fer instance.
WHAAP
Or football.
Hey, Ben-- catch!
Touch-down!
But I'd guess you don't want me to spike you, eh?

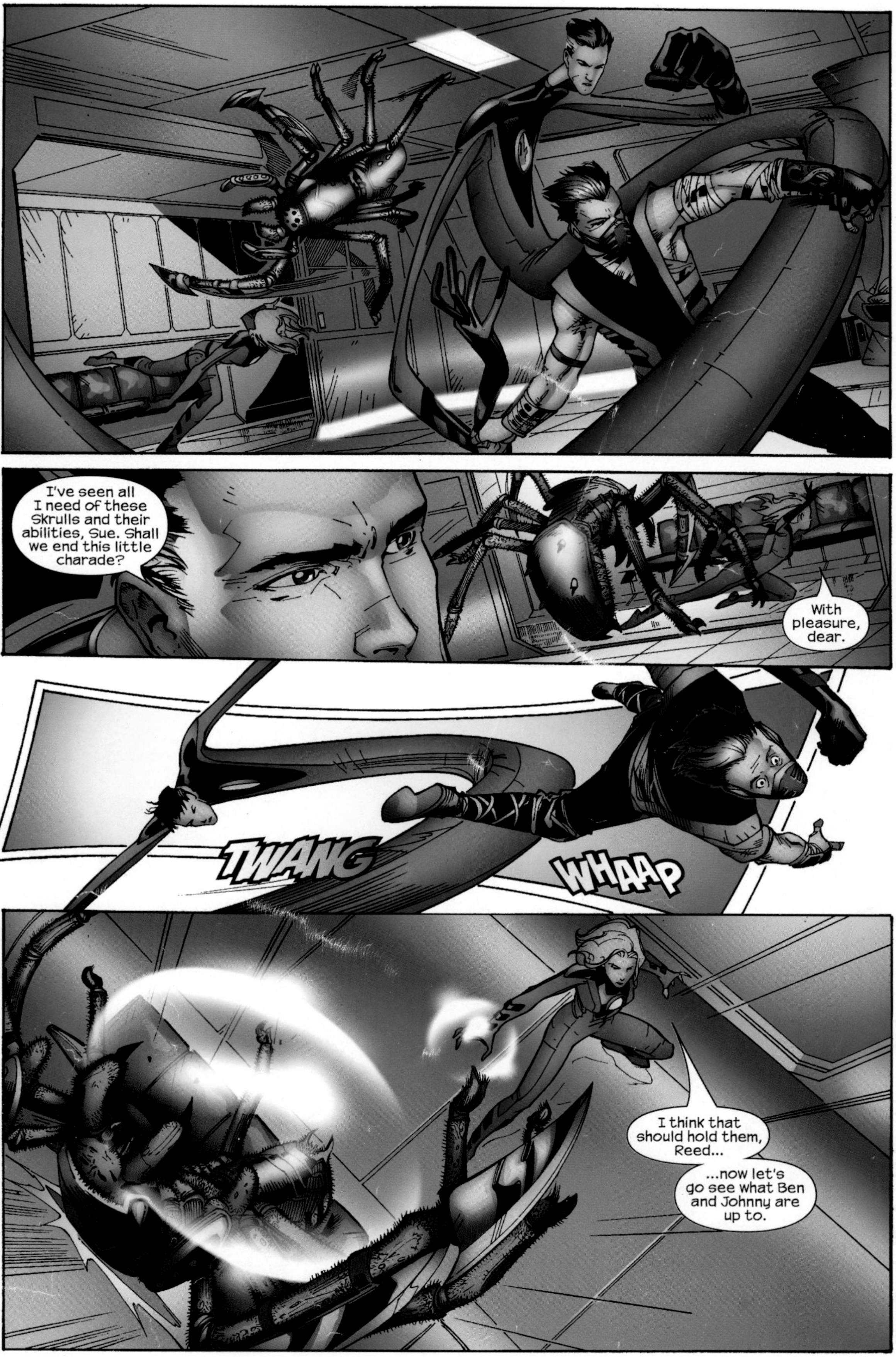

I've seen all I need of these Skrulls and their abilities, Sue. Shall we end this little charade?
With pleasure, dear.
TWANG
WHAAP
I think that should hold them, Reed...
...now let's go see what Ben and Johnny are up to.

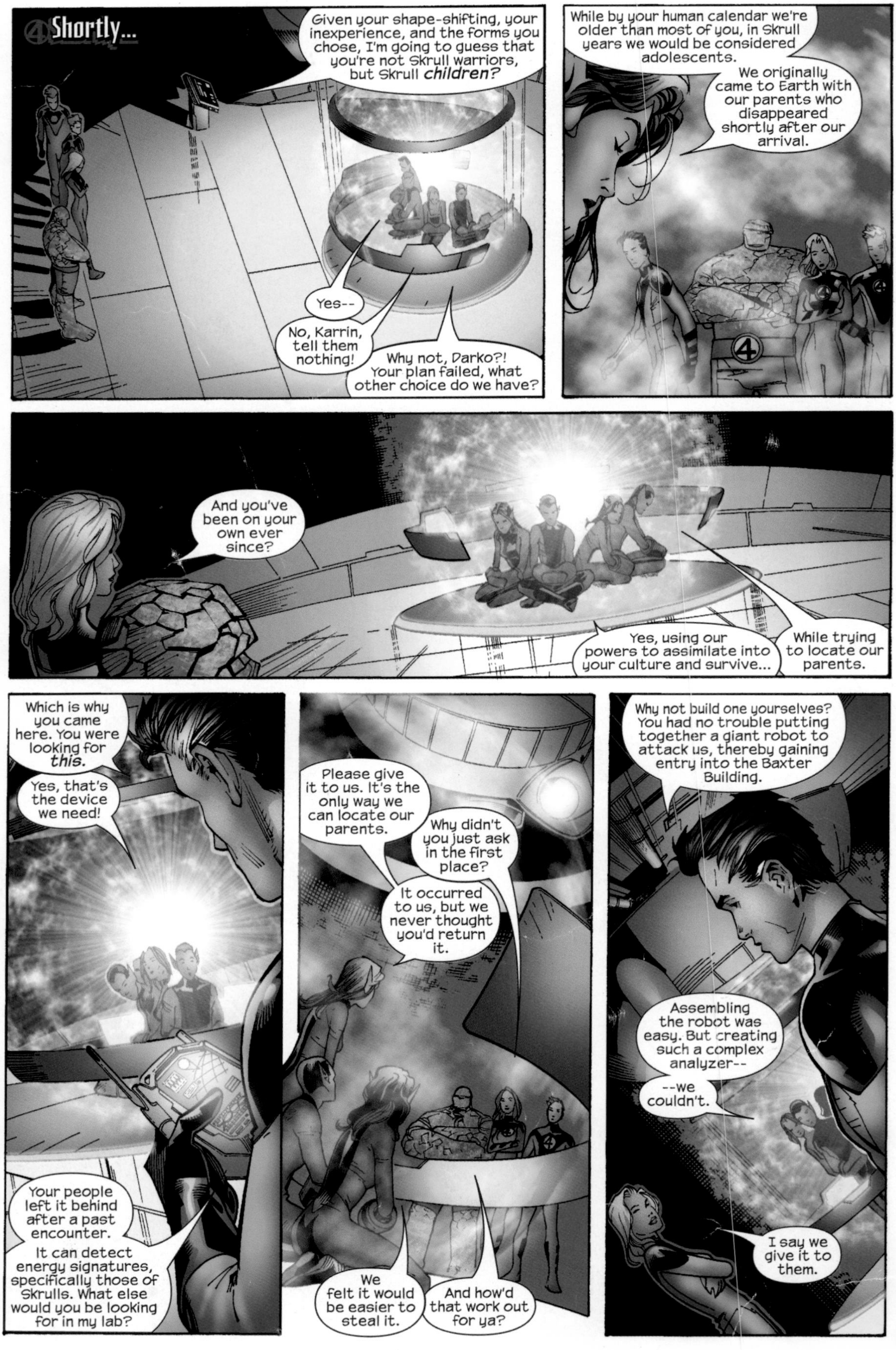
Shortly...
Given your shape-shifting, your inexperience, and the forms you chose, I'm going to guess that you're not Skrull warriors, but Skrull *children*?
Yes--
No, Karrin, tell them nothing!
Why not, Darko?! Your plan failed, what other choice do we have?
While by your human calendar we're older than most of you, in Skrull years we would be considered adolescents.
We originally came to Earth with our parents who disappeared shortly after our arrival.
And you've been on your own ever since?
Yes, using our powers to assimilate into your culture and survive...
While trying to locate our parents.
Which is why you came here. You were looking for *this.*
Yes, that's the device we need!
Your people left it behind after a past encounter.
It can detect energy signatures, specifically those of Skrulls. What else would you be looking for in my lab?
Please give it to us. It's the only way we can locate our parents.
Why didn't you just ask in the first place?
It occurred to us, but we never thought you'd return it.
We felt it would be easier to steal it.
And how'd that work out for ya?
Why not build one yourselves? You had no trouble putting together a giant robot to attack us, thereby gaining entry into the Baxter Building.
Assembling the robot was easy. But creating such a complex analyzer--
--we couldn't.
I say we give it to them.

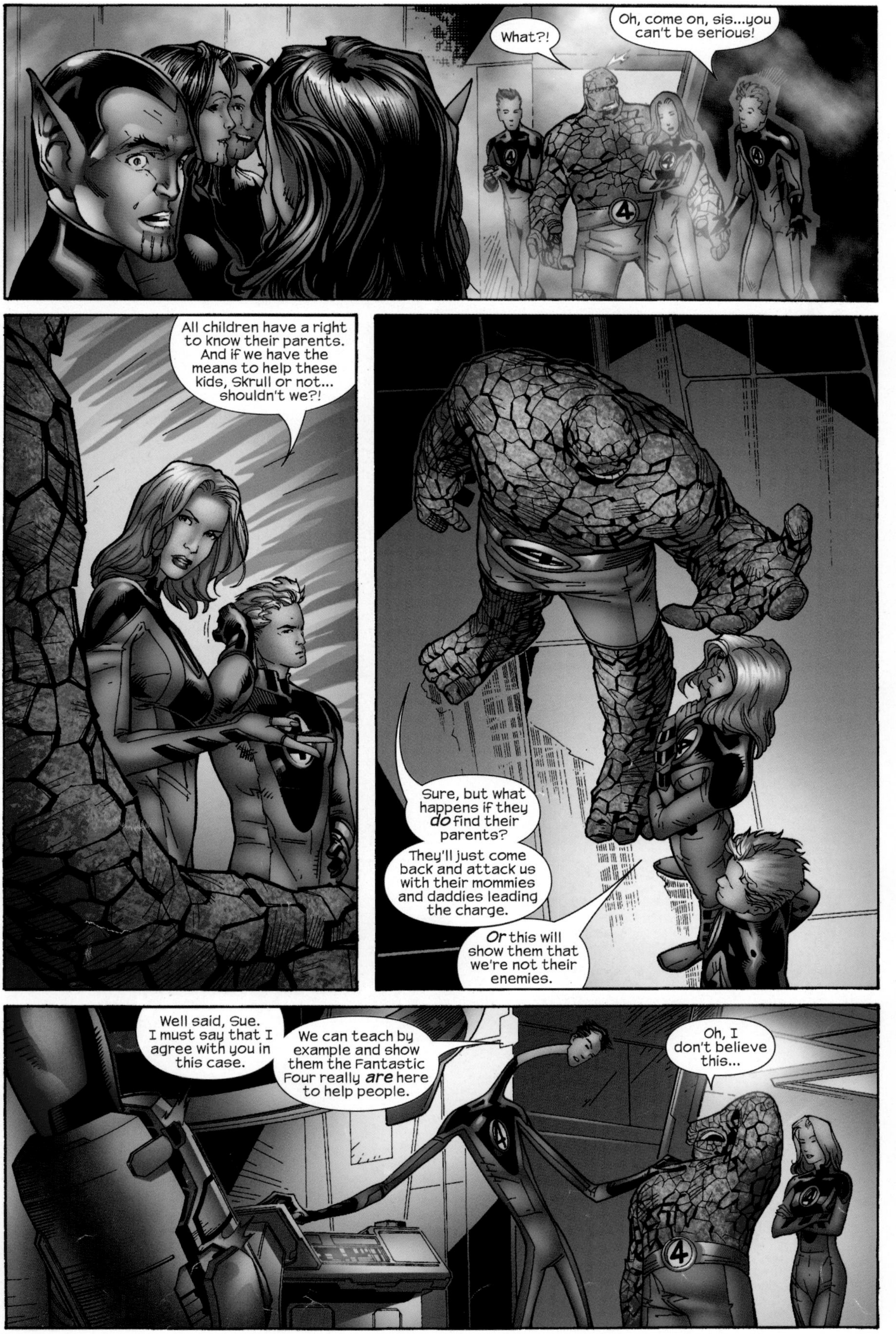

What?!
Oh, come on, sis...you can't be serious!
All children have a right to know their parents. And if we have the means to help these kids, Skrull or not... shouldn't we?!
Sure, but what happens if they *do* find their parents?
They'll just come back and attack us with their mommies and daddies leading the charge.
Or this will show them that we're not their enemies.
Well said, Sue. I must say that I agree with you in this case.
We can teach by example and show them the Fantastic Four really *are* here to help people.
Oh, I don't believe this...

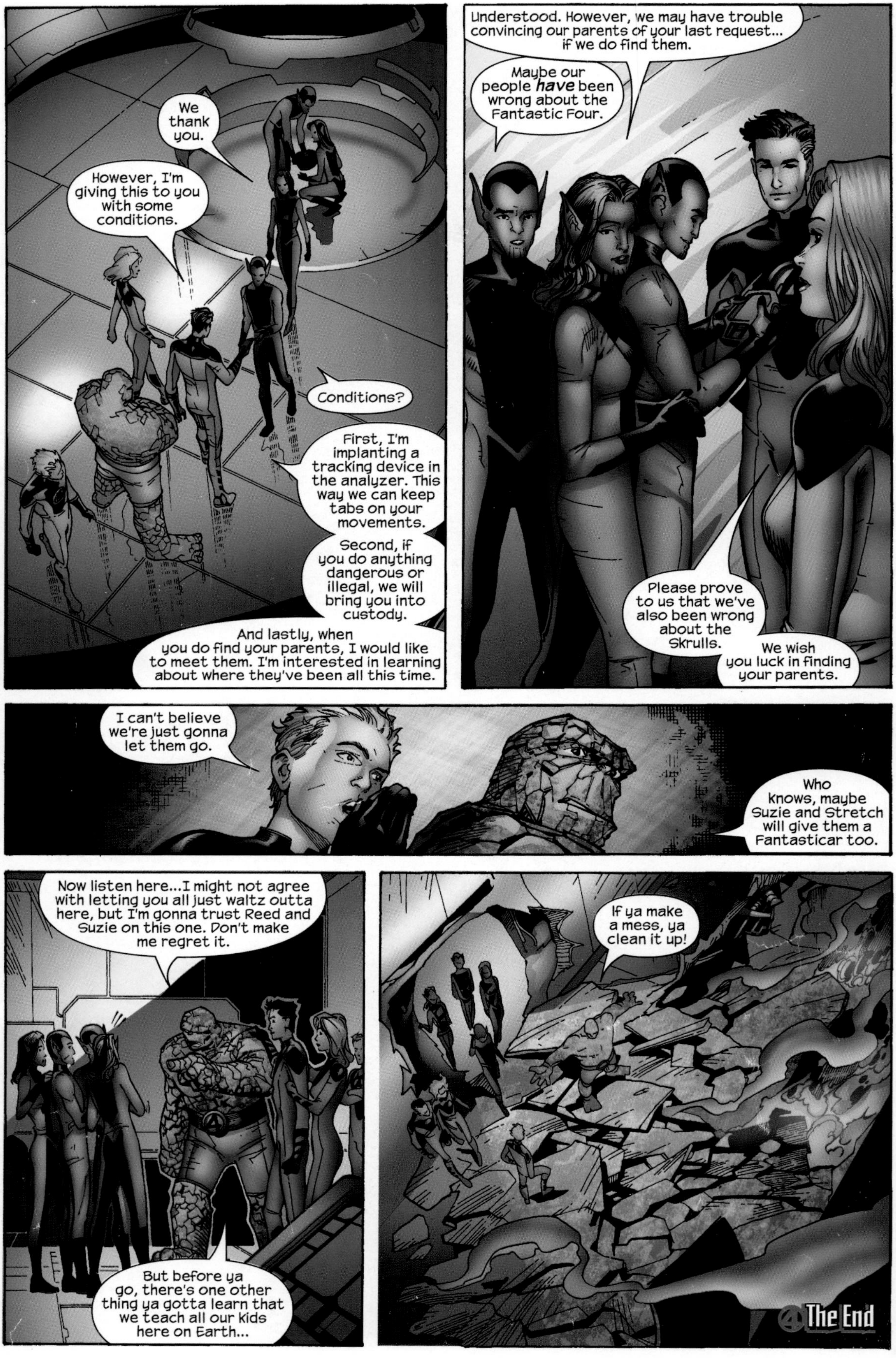
We thank you.
However, I'm giving this to you with some conditions.
Conditions?
First, I'm implanting a tracking device in the analyzer. This way we can keep tabs on your movements.
Second, if you do anything dangerous or illegal, we will bring you into custody.
And lastly, when you do find your parents, I would like to meet them. I'm interested in learning about where they've been all this time.
Understood. However, we may have trouble convincing our parents of your last request... if we do find them.
Maybe our people *have* been wrong about the Fantastic Four.
Please prove to us that we've also been wrong about the Skrulls.
We wish you luck in finding your parents.
I can't believe we're just gonna let them go.
Who knows, maybe Suzie and Stretch will give them a Fantasticar too.
Now listen here...I might not agree with letting you all just waltz outta here, but I'm gonna trust Reed and Suzie on this one. Don't make me regret it.
But before ya go, there's one other thing ya gotta learn that we teach all our kids here on Earth...
If ya make a mess, ya clean it up!
The End

Yoshida, Akira.
Fantastic four in the apple
doesn't fall far

FEB   2007